Destiny's
BIG NEWS

Look for these and other books about Linelle Destiny in the Linelle Destiny Series:

Visit www.thesecretsistersclub.com

Linelle Destiny Series

Destiny's
BIG NEWS

Dr. Alicia Holland
Illustrations by Anoop PC

This book may be ordered through booksellers or by contacting:

iGlobal Educational Services, LLC
13785 Highway 183, Suite 125
Austin, Texas 78750
www.iglobaleducation.com
512-761-5898

Because of the dynamic nature of the Internet, any web addresses or links contained in this book may have changed since publication and may no longer be valid. The views expressed in this work are solely those of the author and do not necessarily reflect the views of the publisher, and the publisher hereby disclaims any responsibility for them.

This is a work of fiction. Names, characters, businesses, places, events, and incidents are either the products of the author's imagination or used in a fictitious manner. Any resemblance to actual persons, living or dead, or actual events is purely coincidental.

Linelle Destiny Series: **Destiny's Big News**

ISBN-13: 978-1-944346-15-7

Acknowledgements

I want to first honor God for placing in my heart to share my story with others. It was He whom brought Karen and I together to manifest this project. I am so grateful for Karen Hendry as she took my notes and helped write this fictitious book. There are truly no words to express my gratitude as you are truly a blessing.

I also want to thank Surendra Gupta for his creativity in formatting and Anoop PC for his creativity in bringing life to the designs and illustrations in this book series. Both of you are amazing!

Dedication

I dedicate this book series to my beautiful and talented daughters, Georgia and Amaiya Johnson. Remember, you are valued, loved, and competent. You are worthy!

Part 1:
On Her Own

Chapter 1

First Week

Destiny has been on her own in Austin for three days and it has been tough. She is feeling homesick. It's especially difficult at night, but she knows she needs to keep moving forward. She decides to place another ad in the local newspaper for her tutoring business. After all, she needs to grow her business and response to the ad she placed a couple of weeks ago wasn't as good as she had hoped.

Now that it is closer to the beginning of the school year, there will be more people looking for help. It's the perfect time to advertise! Destiny goes online and places her ad. It says:

The new school year is about to begin!
Get a head start in Math with...
GET YOUR MIND RIGHT TUTORING
6 years' experience!
Every child has the ability to learn math.
Don't give up! Believe!

After she places the advertisement, Destiny sits and stares at her computer screen. Placing the ad just made her homesickness worse than ever. She knows she needs to do something to help boost her spirits.

Destiny recalls a flyer she saw on the bulletin board in the foyer of her apartment complex. There was something about a movie night and Destiny thinks it was for Friday night.

Destiny goes outside and down the stairs, making her way around the building to the office entrance. Inside, on the bulletin board next to the mailboxes, Destiny sees the flyer. She is right! There is a movie night tonight. They are showing *White Chicks*.

Destiny looks at her cell phone. The movie starts in 15 minutes. Part of her wants to just go back up to her apartment and lay low, but Destiny knows it will do her good to get out and meet some of the neighbors.

She walks down the hallway to the common room for the apartment complex. It's a big room that is available for tenants to host small parties or events. There are chairs and cushions set up all around the room and more than half of them are filled with people who are facing the large TV at the far end of the room.

Destiny doesn't want to go too far toward the front. She is a little nervous about being new here. She chooses a seat close to the back and the woman beside her immediately holds out her hand.

"Howdy," she says. "You're that new tenant, aren't you? Up in 304?"

"Yes, I am. My name's Destiny."

"Pleased to meet you, Destiny," says the woman. "I'm Sharia and this here is Yvette and my boyfriend, Q." Sharia gestures to the two people sitting next to her. Sharia has large beautiful brown eyes that seem to draw a person into her. She looks tall, even though she is sitting down, and her hair is crazy all over the place, yet somehow looks fabulous on her. Yvette seems to be the opposite, a tiny woman with blue eyes and neat hair. Q is wearing a leather jacket and is a big muscular fellow.

Destiny shakes hands with everyone. "Where are you from?" asks Yvette.

"I just moved here from Louisiana," replies Destiny. "I got a teaching job here in Austin."

"Oh, that's right," says Sharia. "They have that hiring freeze going on there, don't they?"

Destiny nods.

"Well, Yvette and I are teachers, too. Welcome to teaching in Austin."

"Thanks," says Destiny. "You're from Texas?"

"Born and raised," replies Sharia.

Destiny is about to ask them where they teach, but the lights are turned off and the movie starts. She sits back and gets ready to enjoy the movie with some new friends.

After the movie that evening, Destiny sees there are a couple of messages on her phone. She is about to check them when she gets a call from Momma. "I'm doing fine, Momma," says Destiny, hoping Momma doesn't catch the lie in her voice. Well, it's only a half-lie. She is doing okay, during the day.

Momma sounds brave, too, but Destiny knows better. There is a sense of concern in her voice, like she's worried that because she can't see Destiny, she isn't certain Destiny is okay. They chat for a couple of minutes.

"Yes, Momma. I will." A pause. "I love you, too. Bye."

After she hangs up from talking to Momma, Destiny checks her messages and is pleased that two people have called to sign up for tutoring and her new ad isn't even up and running, yet.

Just when Destiny thinks she is done for the evening and is on her way to get ready for bed, the phone rings again. This time, it's Alvin. He wants to get together with her tomorrow and they make plans to have dinner. Destiny is so excited that it takes her a while to fall asleep that night.

The next day, Destiny arrives at the restaurant right on time. It's a Jamaican restaurant she has never heard of, but she is excited to try it. She goes in and Alvin is already waiting at a table. He stands up and Destiny is blown away by how handsome he is. He is dressed in jeans, a dark t-shirt, and a black jacket. He is smiling at the sight of her.

Destiny runs and gives Alvin a huge hug. She's glad she decided to wear a dress. It's a simple summer dress, yellow with blue flowers, and she catches Alvin looking her up and down.

"You look great," he says.

"Thanks. So do you." He definitely does. He is slim, like runners tend to be, but he still has some muscular bulk. *Just right*, thinks Destiny.

Alvin pulls out Destiny's chair for her and she sits down. Then he takes his seat and the waitress arrives to take their orders. "May mi help yuh?"

Alvin replies, "Fi mi lady an mi want..." Then Alvin catches the expression on Destiny's face, one of complete and utter confusion, and Destiny can tell he has realized she doesn't understand a word he is saying.

"Right," he says to Destiny, "You don't know Jamaican Patois."

"Jamaican Patois?" asks Destiny.

"It's a form of Creole language," says the waitress, smiling. "Now, what can I get the two of you?"

"We'll both have a ginger beer," says Alvin. "You have to try the ginger beer," he says to Destiny with a wink. "And I'll have the Portland Sample Platter." Destiny looked at the menu and saw that Alvin's dish came with Sticky Citrus Wings, Fried Plantains, and Jerk Shrimp.

She looked for a moment longer and then said, "I'll try the Rude Boy Jerk Chicken Wings, Fried Plantain, and a Jamaican Patty."

"Good choice," says the waitress and Alvin nods his agreement.

"It's so good to see you," says Alvin after the waitress leaves the table.

"I know. It's been way too long," Destiny replies.

"So where will you be teaching?" asks Alvin.

"At Fulkes Middle School. I can't wait to get in there and start working with those kids. It'll be so awesome! Then there is my tutoring business, which I've moved here with me. I have been advertising and people are starting to sign up."

"How long have you been tutoring people?"

"When I was in grade 8 I was tutoring a couple of my friends. Then I worked as assistant during summer school that year and started tutoring kids there. Before I knew it, I had my own tutoring business, Get Your Mind Right Tutoring, and I haven't looked back. It was booming at home, but now I have to start all over here."

"Well," says Alvin, "Austin is a big place and you are a talented woman. I am sure your tutoring business will boom even louder here than it did back home."

"Thanks," says Destiny, blushing under Alvin's praise. "Enough about me. What about you? What have you been up to, besides racing, of course?"

Alvin chuckles. "Yes, I've been racing a lot, but I want to settle down and focus on some other projects I've been wanting to take on."

"Yeah, like what?" asks Destiny.

"Well, I want to start an annual 5K race here in Austin. I think it would be really nice to encourage more people to take up running."

"That sounds great," says Destiny as their food arrives. I think people would really go for that. But what else? You said *projects*." Destiny emphasizes the last word.

"I plan to start a clothing line called 'No EGO,' which means No Edging God Out. It will be sporty and comfortable, but nice-looking clothing. What do you think?"

Destiny is impressed. She has an immediate vision of Alvin firing the starting pistol at his first 5K race and then the vision changes to show him introducing the debut selection of his new clothing line. He is beaming and she knows it will come true.

"Hello, earth to Destiny," says Alvin. "What do you think?"

"I think it's a fabulous idea! And I love the name."

Then they start eating their wings. Destiny's concerns about the wings being too hot are soon alleviated. Despite the fact that she had heard how spicy Jamaican food is, the wings aren't spicy at all. She loves them and happily digs in. They are messy, though, and she is glad the waitress left extra napkins and wet wipes.

With good food and Alvin as company, Destiny settles in and enjoys talking with Alvin about their future plans. It is a perfect evening and Destiny sighs with contentment as their plates are cleared away.

"Dessert?" asks Alvin.

"I don't know if I can eat anymore."

"We could share."

Destiny considers this. "Okay, let's do it."

They choose a wonderful Jamaican Run Cake and enjoy it immensely. Destiny can't eat all of her half, but Alvin is happy to finish it. Then, Alvin orders another Jamaican Patty to eat while they are waiting for the bill.

"You're still hungry?" Destiny is shocked.

"Always," replies Alvin.

"May I try a piece?"

"Sorry, but this one is all mine," says Alvin with a grin. The man has an appetite, thinks Destiny. It is a magical evening.

Chapter 2

First Day

D estiny has been living on the memory of dinner with
Alvin. It has been getting her through her lonely evenings. That and the thought of the new school year
starting. Fortunately, Destiny is heading into the school today
to get herself set up and ready to go for the new school year.
School starts next week and she just wants everything to go
perfectly.

When Destiny arrives at the school, she goes into the office
and asks the secretary if she can see Dr. Easton. Dr. Easton is
the principal of the school and Destiny feels it is best if she
speaks with him personally to meet him and find out where her
classroom is.

"Sure, sugar," says the woman behind the desk. "And
you are?"

"I'm the new teacher, Destiny Sycamores."

"Oh, yes," she says, peering over her glasses at Destiny as if
she's trying to size her up. "He's just in there." She nods toward
a door to Destiny's right. Destiny walks over and knocks on the

door frame. Although the door is open, she waits at the threshold until she is invited in with a crisp, "Come in."

"Hello," says Destiny, walking into the office. "I'm Destiny Sycamores, your new teacher."

"Ah, yes," says Dr. Easton, looking up from his computer. "My new teacher that I didn't really hire."

"Pardon me?" says Destiny.

"I'm sorry," Dr. Easton says, standing up and extending his hand. Destiny shakes it, his grip firm and his skin so dry it almost feels scaly. Then he gestures to the chair beside Destiny and she takes a seat.

"You see, I understand that you were hired to teach at this school and I appreciate that," says Dr. Easton, reseating himself. "I understand you are highly qualified and talented, too. The problem is that I had no knowledge of this hire until two days ago. I had been away and since I wasn't actually the one who interviewed and hired you and it was done in Lousiana... Well, as you can imagine it came as quite a surprise when I got back to the office."

"Oh, yes. Well, I can understand that," says Destiny. "But I do still have the job?"

"Oh, yes, you have the job," says Dr. Easton. "The problem is you have a job without a classroom."

"Oh, I see. What does that mean, exactly?"

"It means that for now you will have to go to your students instead of them coming to you."

"I see," says Destiny again, as Dr. Easton holds a piece of paper out for her.

"This is a map of the school." Then he takes the map back, marks an X on one spot and hands it back to Destiny. "You're here and your first class of the day will be in this room. It would be a good idea to familiarize yourself with the school layout before next week."

"Yes," Destiny agrees. "And where can I work for now, to prepare for my classes?"

"There is a supplemental education office here on the second floor." He points to a spot on the map. "You can make use of that for the rest of this week."

Dr. Easton sits down at his computer again, making it obvious that their initial meeting is over. Destiny stands up and walks out of his office. Then she stands in the main office for a few moments, getting her bearings.

"You can find your way okay?" asks the secretary.

"Oh, yes," says Destiny. "I'm good with maps... uh?"

"So sorry, darlin'. I didn't tell you my name, did I?"

Destiny shakes her head.

"I'm Sara Honeywell, school secretary for the past 12 years," she says proudly. "Run a tight ship here, I do. And don't you worry about a thing. We'll find a classroom for you soon enough."

"Thank you," says Destiny. "Well, I had better get to work. Only a couple of days to get ready."

Mrs. Honeywell nods and Destiny sets off to tour around the school.

The following Monday, Destiny arrives at school early. She wants to be there in enough time to make a good impression. Maybe Dr. Easton has even found a classroom for her already. But when she gets there and looks hopefully at Mrs. Honeywell, she shakes her head. No such luck.

Destiny's first class of the day is teaching Math Intervention to a grade seven class. Destiny feels right at home when she meets her students and begins teaching. One of her students raises his hand and Destiny acknowledges him. "Where are you from, Miss Sycamores? You don't sound like you're from around here."

"No, I'm not, Jeb, and thank you for noticing. I'm from Many, Louisiana. Just moved here last month to come and teach you lovely folks."

Other students start asking Destiny questions. One girl raises her hand and when Destiny calls on her she asks her if Destiny likes it in Texas.

"Oh, yes," says Destiny, "very much. Although, I do miss my family back home."

"They aren't that far away, though, are they Miss Sycamores?" says a boy in the front row. "Many, Louisiana is only about 300 hundred miles away."

"Why, yes it is," says Destiny. "You're David, right?" He nods. "You must be good with maps and distances."

"Yes, ma'am."

Destiny gets back to the math lesson and enjoys the rest of the period. It's only when she gets to her next class, her grade 8 Math Intervention, that she has a more challenging time. She has to hurry to get there because it's two floors up. Then she finds that six of the nine students in her class can't speak a word of English. Thankfully, Spanish is their language and even more thankfully, Destiny took high school Spanish and can get by well enough in the language. It takes her a while to get the hang of it, though. She doesn't speak Spanish often.

Before Destiny knows it, the school day is at an end. She so enjoyed meeting her students and she is quite chipper as she walks down the hall and pushes the down button for the elevator. She sees the English teacher she met earlier, Steph Lawson.

"Going down?" Destiny asks.

"No, thanks," says Steph. "I always take the stairs. More exercise." She winks and disappears into the stairwell.

Destiny gets in the elevator and it begins its decent. But it doesn't go far before it lurches to a stop. Destiny stumbles and then regains her footing. She wonders what is going on and tries to push the button for the main floor. Nothing happens. So, Destiny pushes the button for the second floor, then the third. Then she tries all the buttons, including the one to open the doors. Nothing works.

"I should have taken the stairs with Steph," Destiny mutters to herself. Then she begins to panic and fans herself with the papers she is holding in her hand. "Calm down," she says.

She pushes the button of the emergency intercom and speaks into it. "Hello? Hello? If anyone can hear me, this is Destiny Sycamores and I'm stuck in the elevator. Hello?"

There is no response. It's just about the end of the school day and Destiny figures someone will try to use the elevator soon and figure out it isn't working.

Destiny sits down and breathes deeply, willing herself to stay calm. She is getting hot in that little elevator and it doesn't take long for the drab beige walls to become boring to stare at. At least the lights are still working.

Destiny listens to the silence getting louder and louder. She had heard the expression 'deafening silence' before, but never really understood it until now. Stuck in this elevator, she can barely stand the silence.

Finally, Destiny tries the intercom again. Nothing. She takes out some papers and starts reading through them, trying to take her mind off things. Then she thinks of her cell phone, but remembers it doesn't pick up a signal in elevators. She tries anyway, but nothing.

After what feels like an eternity, Destiny gets to the point where she thinks she might die in that elevator. They will finally realize it's stuck and pry open the doors and she will be nothing but a lifeless husk. They will erect a plaque in her honor and she will always be remembered as the teacher they never got to know before her untimely death somewhere between the second and third floors.

Finally, Destiny shakes herself out of her miserable thoughts and tries the buttons again. When they don't work, she tries the intercom again. Mrs. Honeywell answers.

"Hello, dearie."

"Mrs. Honeywell? Oh, thank goodness. It's Destiny Sycamores, the new teacher? I'm stuck in the elevator."

"Sweetie, just call me Sara. And yes, we have someone on their way here now. Should have you out in a jiff."

Sara's jiff turns out to be a half an hour. Finally, Destiny feels the elevator begin to move again. Down, down it goes until it comes to rest on the main floor.

When the doors open, there is Sara, Dr. Easton, a few students, and a man Destiny knows must be the technician. He's wearing those technician-type overalls. "Are you alright?" asks Dr. Easton.

"Yes, thanks. I'm fine," says Destiny. "Glad to be out of there, though."

Sara moves in. "Those darn faulty wires. Now, you just come along and we'll get you a drink of water. Don't want you dehydrating on us now. You'll shrivel up like a raisin, you will."

Destiny allows herself to be led away and has a nice drink of water. She was parched. She thanks Sara and gets ready to leave for the day, despite Sara insisting she stay a while longer to make sure she's fine.

Once Destiny gets out into the fresh air, she takes in a deep breath and smiles. It's so nice to be outside in the sun. As she walks to her car, Destiny decides she is now a stairs person.

Chapter 3

New Friends

Destiny drops her things on the table when she gets home from work. She has been teaching for a couple of weeks now and is getting the hang of things, although not having her own classroom and moving around constantly is tiring. But she is grateful she has a job and pushes those thoughts out of her head.

While it is tempting to just go have a hot bath and curl up with a good book and relax, Destiny knows she has things to do. She checks her messages and finds she has quite a few. Five minutes later, she has written down messages from eight different people looking for tutoring help.

Destiny is amazed. She had been so worried about building her tutoring business, but it seems to be taking on a life of its own and flourishing. Destiny gets a cup of tea and gets ready to start calling all the people who left messages. It will take a while so she might as well get comfortable.

She starts calling and soon has four new students that will be starting next week. She hasn't called all of them yet, but she is getting hungry. "I need a break," she says to herself.

She gets up and gets some leftover soup. While she is waiting for her soup to heat up in the microwave, the phone rings. Thinking it is another new client, she plans to let it go to voicemail, but then she glances at the number and the caller ID shows the name K. Milestone.

Destiny picks up the phone and answers it. "Hello."

"Hi, Destiny. It's Keenan, Keenan Milestone."

"Hi, Keenan. How are you?"

"I'm great," he says. "Listen, I thought I'd give you a quick call to let you know I'm living in Austin now. Dad gave me your number so I could touch base with you."

"That's great Keenan! How is Mr. Milestone?"

"Awe, he's doing just fine. Business is as good as ever, but he sure does miss you. You were his best employee, you know?"

"That's kind of you to say," says Destiny. "So, what brought you to Austin?"

"Work, just like you. Got a job with a company in town."

"That's great!"

"Well, I should let you go," says Keenan. "I just want to get in touch, let you know I'm here, a familiar face from home. I know how hard it is moving away."

"Thank you, Keenan. We should get together sometime and chat over lunch or dinner."

"That would be super. Talk at ya later, Destiny."

"Bye," says Destiny.

Destiny hangs up and gets her soup. She is happy to have heard from Keenan and happy that someone from home lives so close.

The next day at work, Destiny is heading out of her last class before lunch and she nearly runs right into one of the teachers she met briefly last week at the faculty meet and greet.

"Hi," says Destiny. "Sorry about that. I should watch where I'm going. It's Miss Suzette, right?"

"Call me Mal. You're Destiny, right?"

"Yes. Is that Mal short for Mallory?"

Mal nods.

"That's my mother's name," says Destiny.

"How cool is that," says Mal. "Listen, I was just heading out for lunch. You wanna join me? There is a little diner a couple blocks down."

"Yeah, I'd like that."

"Great! I'll meet you in front of the office in five."

Destiny heads down right away. Without a classroom, she pretty much carries her work with her. A couple of minutes later, Mal comes walking down the hall and says, "Shall we?"

It's been raining out, but the streets are drying up. Destiny and Mal dodge the puddles as they walk down the sidewalk. A little girl they pass splashes in the puddles while her mother watches.

"Remember when life was that simple?" asks Mal.

"Barely," replies Destiny.

They go into the diner and grab a booth near the back. The waitress brings them water and takes their drink order. "Ice tea for me," says Mal.

"Same," says Destiny. Then they look at the menu. They don't talk much while they choose lunch and when the waitress comes back with their drinks, they order. Destiny gets a club sandwich and Mal orders a veggie burger.

"You're a vegetarian?" asks Destiny.

"Yup, vegan actually. They say you only live once, generally when talking about eating something bad for you. If I only get to live once, then I would prefer to live a longer and healthier life."

Destiny nods. "I'd love some vegan recipes from you, if you don't mind."

"Sure!"

"So, how long have you been at the school?"

"This is my first year, too," says Mal. "I guess I'm the lucky one who got the classroom."

"You're telling me," says Destiny. "I don't where I'm going half the time. It's hard without a home base."

The food arrives and they dig in. They have to eat quickly because they have to be back at the school in 20 minutes.

"So where are you from?" asks Mal.

"Louisiana. You?"

"South Dakota. I like it here, though. It's got a nice feel to it."

They chat a while longer and then pay the bill and leave. On the way back to the school, Mal says, "You know a few of us from work get together on Wednesday evenings. We call it Working Women's Wednesday. You should come out tonight. We're doing karaoke so you have to bring your voice."

"Sure, I'd like that. Although I don't know about singing."

"Awesome! I'll write down the details and leave them in your mailbox."

They get back to the school and part ways. Destiny has a busy afternoon ahead of her.

Destiny shows up at the Karaoke Ranch, a cute place that is just a few minutes away from her apartment. She goes inside and starts looking around.

"Can I help you?" says a tall man from behind the bar. He has a very deep voice and an accent that sounds like he's from up north, maybe Boston.

"No, I don't think so. I'm just looking for some friends."

"Teachers?"

Destiny nods.

"They're over there." He points to the far left and Destiny sees Mal at a table, along with a couple of other women she recognizes.

"Thanks," says Destiny.

She walks over to the table and Mal speaks up. "Destiny, you made it! Have a seat!"

As Destiny sits down, Mal introduces her to the other women at the table. "Destiny, this is Katie. Did you guys meet already?"

"Sort of," says Katie, the woman to Destiny's right. "At the staff meeting, but it's nice to meet you again, properly this time."

"And this is Julie," says Mal.

"Nice to meet you," shouts Julie from across the table as the music starts to get louder.

"You're just in time," says Mal. They're just getting the music going."

Destiny orders a drink and settles in to listen to people sing. Someone gets up and sings Michael Jackson's 'Beat It' and she's not that bad. Then another woman gets up and sings David Bowie's 'Under Pressure.' It's pretty funny.

Then Mal jumps up. "My turn," she says. "You want to join me, Destiny?"

"I don't know if I could ever do that," Destiny replies.

"You mean you've never done karaoke before?" asks Katie.

"Nope," says Destiny.

Mal points to the display by the stage. "Then you need to go pick a song and get up there."

"Oh, I don't know," says Destiny. "I've never sung anything in front of people before."

Mal shrugs her shoulders and goes up. She starts singing a great rendition of Britney Spears 'Oops... I Did It Again."

Then part way through the song, Mal calls Destiny up on stage to sing the song with her. "Best way to get over the jitters is to jump right in," she whispers.

When the song is over, Mal holds up her hand to signal for Destiny to stay on the stage. Then she goes down and chooses another song. The music starts and Destiny starts clapping. She is feeling fine and she can handle this because they are playing her song – Miley Cyrus' 'Party In The U.S.A.'! She sings her heart out.

When the song is done, Destiny feels alive! She goes back to the table and everyone congratulates her on her performance. "You slayed that song!" says Julie.

"It was so fun!" says Destiny. "I can't believe I did that!"

Destiny will remember this night forever. Plus, she can't wait to tell her family all about it, especially Michelle. Michelle would be proud of her little sister for letting loose! Destiny sits back and enjoys the rest of the evening getting to know her new friends.

Part 2
Success!

Chapter 4

Math Class

It's a stunning October day and Destiny arrives at the school in a splendid mood. The southern heat has relaxed a little and the air is mild and pleasant. When she gets into the office and is checking her mailbox Sara walks in and trills, "Oh good, Destiny. Principal Easton wants to see you! Some exciting news."

"Is it a classroom?" asks Destiny, hope clearly showing on her face because Sara smiles.

"Maybe," says Sara and she winks.

Destiny goes over and knocks on Principal Easton's door. She is happy at the prospect of having a classroom of her own, but she wonders how they managed to find one for her. "Come in," he calls.

Destiny walks in and he looks up from the form he is filling out on his desk. "Ah, prefect, Miss Sycamores. I have some good news for you. We have found you a classroom!"

"That's great, Principal Easton. I hope you didn't go to too much trouble to figure out where to put me."

"To be honest, it wasn't any trouble at all on our part. A classroom has opened up because one of our teachers is leaving."

"Oh, really? Who?" asks Destiny. She starts to get a horrible feeling in her stomach. She is benefitting from someone else leaving. She hopes they are going to something better and this is good for everyone.

"Miss Suzette will be taking her leave from her position."

"Permanently?" Destiny blurts out. She hadn't heard a word of this from Mal. What is going on?

"Yes, I'm afraid so."

"May I ask why?"

Principal Easton sighs. "All I can say is that the board felt she wasn't performing to the standards we need. She has been struggling to effectively deliver material and teach the grade seven and eight ESL students. For this reason, you will be taking over her 7th and 8th grade math classes. You'll be starting today."

The awful feeling in the pit of Destiny's stomach grows ice cold and her heart begins to thump. She knew Mal was having a hard time communicating the work to her class, but she didn't know it was that bad. Poor Mal.

Destiny thanks Principal Easton and assures him the grade seven and eight ESL math classes are in good hands. Then she heads upstairs to her new classroom. She has to get something together for that day and hopes Mal has left some indication as to where she left off in her teaching.

Destiny is surprised to find Mal in the classroom, packing up the last of her personal items. "Oh. Hi, Mal. I didn't realize you were still here."

Mal looks up at Destiny. She flashes a forced smile, but her eyes are like daggers. "Just finishing up. I'll be out of your way in a minute."

"Don't be silly, Mal," says Destiny. "You're not in my way. Listen, I'm so sorry this happened. I only just found out now, before coming upstairs."

"Yeah, well, that's how it goes."

"Do you need any help?" asks Destiny.

"No, I'm done. I left my lesson plan for the day on your desk." Mal's emphasis of the word "your" stings Destiny.

"Thank you," says Destiny and then Mal is gone. Destiny feels so sad because Mel was becoming such a good friend. Surely she knows Destiny had nothing to do with this. Destiny can only hope Mal will forgive and forget.

A half an hour later, Destiny's class starts filing into the room. She says hello to the students. "Hi everyone. I am Miss Sycamores, your new teacher."

The students are in the process of taking their seats and they stop and stare at Destiny. One of them speaks up. "Where is Miss Suzette?"

Destiny considered what to say to the students before they arrived because she knew someone would ask. She wanted to make it clear that Mal wasn't coming back, but tell them in a way that didn't make Mal look bad.

"The school board has decided that she has talents that are needed elsewhere, so they have given me her classes and moved her to a different school." At least, Destiny hopes that last part is true.

"Where?" asks another student.

"That I don't know," says Destiny. "Now, if you will all take your seats, we can get started."

Despite what Destiny said, the students start talking to each other. Destiny can see them shaking their heads and she catches snippets, such as, "Miss Suzette was a great teacher... ...perfect for this class... I'll miss her..."

The day was trying and the following two weeks in the class continued to be. Every day when Destiny came in, she had a very difficult time getting the students' attention so she could with them. They seemed to resist everything she did. Spitballs flew through the classroom with amazing speed and notes were passed around almost as quickly. It was clear they were not happy with the change.

One day, Destiny feels she is at the end of her rope. She knows she needs to do something to get through to the students, so after class one day she calls one of her students over to her desk. "Hi Jake."

"Hi," he responds, fidgeting and looking back toward the door, through which his friends have already passed.

"Listen," says Destiny. "I understand you and some of the others play basketball."

"Yeah, so what?" He shakes his dark bangs out of his eyes.

"Well, I was wondering when your next game is because I want to come out and see you play."

"You do?" Jake's eyes widen in surprise.

"Yes," replies Destiny. "It's important to me to keep up with my students and support them in all areas of their lives. Plus, I love basketball. I used to play, you know."

"Uh, cool," says Jake. "Well, the next game is tomorrow."

"Wonderful," says Destiny. "I'll see you there!"

The following day, Destiny is true to her word and she enjoys the game so much. She has some very talented players in her class.

By mid-November, Destiny is finally seeing the results of her efforts. She is beginning to bond with her students and they are beginning to open up and work with her. She is seeing them learn at a phenomenal pace, even the ones who can't speak any English at all.

One day after school, Destiny is sitting at her desk, going over the suggestions her students gave her for a new project she is working on with her class, when Julie comes in.

Julie also works with the ESL students, and over the past few weeks, Destiny and Julie have become good friends. Julie knows Destiny had nothing to do with what happened to Mal. "Mal did that to herself," Julie would say.

"Hey, Destiny. What's up? You ready to get out of here?"

"Almost," replies Destiny. "Just looking over these suggestions of what we can sell in out Fabulous Favorites store."

"So, Easton said yes?"

"He did!" exclaims Destiny. "I was worried he might not, but I think he is happy with the results I'm getting from the students and the fact that they are excited about the project. Now, I am making up a shopping list so I can get the things we are planning to sell. We'll be open for business on Monday!"

"That's awesome!" says Julie.

"Yeah. Mike and Yvonne are even going to advertise the store in the morning announcements on Monday.

The students are doing it as part of their Theater Arts assignment."

"Cool. What are you guys going to sell in this store?"

"Oh, you know knick knacks. Erasers, cool pencils, funky bracelets, other things the students are interested in."

"Glitter pens?" asks Julie.

"Definitely glitter pens," replies Destiny.

"Sounds like I should do some shopping there, myself," says Julie. "You wanna grab a bite?"

"Sorry, I can't today," says Destiny. "Too much to do."

"You always have too much to do," Julie shoots back, but with a smile on her face. "What are you doing, going for teacher of the year or something?"

"Nope, just enjoying my class and my job," says Destiny.

"Well, you need to come out soon."

"I will," says Destiny.

"Bye," says Julie as she walks out the door.

Destiny is packing up and checks to make sure there is enough room in the cupboard for the merchandise when she brings it in over the weekend. As she closes up, she all of a sudden sees an even bigger store.

It's a vision of a Secret Sisters Club store. It's in a real store space, with a sign above the door, and it's filled with all sorts of great stuff.

Destiny smiles to herself, full of the knowledge she will have that store one day. But if she is going to plan it, then she needs to get working on the Secret Sisters Club. Time is tight, but she will find a way because it's so important. Maybe she won't be going out with Julie any time soon. Her weekends are filling up!

Chapter 5

Master's Degree

I t is a big day for Destiny. She has been given the day off of work because she will be defending her Master's degree thesis at 9:30 am. She sits at home on a February morning waiting for the phone to ring as she doodles on a piece of paper.

Her stomach is in knots. Part of her is glad she isn't actually in Louisiana defending her thesis in person because she would probably feel more nervous, but at the same time, it feels strange to be doing it over the phone. The reality is that she wasn't able to take enough time off work to travel back to Louisiana to defend, so the conference call was the only solution.

The phone rings at 9:31 am, which really isn't late, but Destiny feels like she has been waiting forever for the call. She answers the phone, "Hello?"

"Hi, Destiny," says Dr. Gino, Destiny's thesis supervisor. "How are you?"

"I'm good, Dr. Gino. How are you?"

"I'm fine, Destiny. As for you, I know you're nervous. Remember, I've been where you are before. But you'll do just fine. You know your stuff and you are brilliant when it comes to your students and what they need. This will be a piece of cake."

"Thank you," says Destiny. "I hope you're right."

"I know I am. Now, give me a moment to get Dr. Adderley on the line." There is silence for a minute or so and then Dr. Gino is back. "Destiny, Dr. Adderley is now on the line."

Dr. Adderley is another professor and is on Destiny's thesis committee. She has met him a couple of times and he always seems so intimidating. Destiny prays to herself that she doesn't mess up.

"Hi, Dr. Adderley," says Destiny.

"Hello, Destiny," Dr. Adderley replies. "I am looking forward to hearing you defend today. Shall, we proceed?"

"Yes, please," says Destiny. I just want to get this over with, she thinks.

With that, Destiny spends 20 minutes giving her thesis presentation, with only the occasional comment or request for clarification from either Dr. Gino or Dr. Adderley. When she is finished, Destiny spends another hour and a quarter answering questions the two professors ask of her. It is a gruelling process, one she is happy to have come to an end.

Finally, Dr. Gino says, "Destiny, I think that is all the questions we have for you. Are you in agreement, Dr. Adderley?"

"Yes, I am."

"Great," says Dr. Gino. "Destiny, please give us just a couple of minutes to deliberate and then we will get you back on the line."

"Yes, okay," says Destiny. While she is waiting, she paces around her living room. Two minutes seems like an hour, and when the call comes back on, Destiny sucks in her breath.

"Hello, Destiny," says Dr. Gino. "Are you there?"

"Yes," says Destiny, realizing she was holding her breath.

"We are happy to tell you that you have passed your Master's thesis and will graduate at the convocation in May. Congratulations!"

"Yes, congratulations, Destiny," adds Dr. Adderley. "Your thesis was very impressive."

"Thank you both so much," says Destiny. "I am so happy you liked it."

"Well, Destiny," says Dr. Adderley, "you deserve everything you get because you have excelled at your work. I wish you the best with the rest of your school year."

"Thank you," replies Destiny.

With that, Dr. Adderley says goodbye and hangs up. Dr. Gino says, "He's right, Destiny. You are very bright and you have a promising future. I wish you were here so I could take you out to dinner to celebrate."

"Thank you, Dr. Gino. I think I will take myself out to lunch."

"You do that, dear. Good bye and all the best."

"Bye," says Destiny.

Destiny can't help grinning from ear to ear as she gets ready to go out. What a great day!

Destiny goes to bed that night happier than she has ever been. Sometime through the night, she dreams. She is walking next to palm trees and crystal blue water in a graduation gown. The sound of the ocean water lapping the shore is soothing. Next thing she knows, she is standing among other graduates and someone calls to her, saying, "Dr. Sycamores, will you please come forward."

Destiny wakes up with her heart pounding. What a fabulous dream! No one in her family has ever been called Dr. before, unless you count her brothers calling themselves Dr. Love or saying the Love Doctor is in when they were around their friends.

One of Destiny's old friends, Trent, used to call himself the Street Doctor. Destiny giggles at the thought of it. She has no idea why he would want to be called the Street Doctor as he was far more capable of being an excellent Love Doctor as far as she can remember.

Destiny thinks about her dream. It's about her getting her doctorate degree in education. She lays there thinking about it for a while, her mind busy with the possibilities. She knows that her dream will come true. Getting her PhD is Destiny's next big goal.

Eventually Destiny falls back to sleep with thoughts of a potential PhD project running through her head like sheep. Except, she isn't counting; she is running after them.

The next day, when Destiny arrives at school, there are flowers waiting for her and a sign in the staff room that says congratulations. There is even a cake to celebrate. Principal Easton, Sara, and the teachers all congratulate Destiny on achieving her Master's degree.

As they have some cake in the staff room before class starts, Destiny says to Principal Easton, "This is all wonderful, thank you, but how did you know I would be successful?"

"Now, Miss Sycamores," says Principal Easton. "Do you really think you could have possibly failed?"

"Maybe," says Destiny.

"I highly doubt it," he says. "Anyway, I also wanted to ask you if you would be interested in attending an education conference. It's in Arizona in March. It would be a great learning experience for you and they have some great sessions on working with ESL students that I think would benefit your teaching and the students in this school."

"Yes," says Destiny. "I'd like that very much!"

"Wonderful, he says. "It's settled, then."

A few minutes later, Destiny is heading back upstairs to her classroom. She walks up the stairs with Julie.

Julie asks, "What were you and Principal Easton talking about for such a long time?"

"Well, he was congratulating me and then he asked me to attend a conference next month in Arizona."

"Oh, really?" Julie says a little stiffly. "That's great."

"Yes, I'm excited," says Destiny. "I've never been to a conference before. Anyway, I'll talk to you later."

Destiny ducks into her classroom and heads toward her desk, as happy as she can be. Then she notices the cabinet in which to Fabulous Favorites merchandise is stored in sitting open and empty.

Destiny goes over to the cabinet and can see that the doors were pried open. Everything is gone! It must have happened yesterday, when there was a supply teacher filling in for Destiny.

Destiny closes the doors to the cabinet as best she can. They won't shut properly because they are bent. As her students start filing in, she goes and stands behind her desk. When everyone is seated, Destiny takes attendance. Then she tells them the bad news.

"I'm sorry to say that someone broke into our Fabulous Favorites cabinet and stole everything. We have nothing to sell now, so we'll have to close down the store."

There was an eruption of groans and disappointment from the students. "Who would do such a thing?" asks Yvonne.

"I don't know," answers Destiny. "But it certainly wasn't very nice. I just want you all to know that you all did a wonderful job of running it while we had it open. I am proud of all of you and you should all be proud of yourselves."

At that, the class claps and cheers, but they are also very disappointed. So is Destiny. Despite her own personal happiness, she can't help but feel bad for her students. They worked so hard to make that store a success.

Chapter 6
Tutoring

One Friday evening in early March, Destiny gets home late from tutoring. She has seen five different clients since school got out that day and only just managed to get time for a bite to eat while on the go. It has become increasingly difficult and time-consuming to drive around and see all of her clients. It is clear to Destiny that it is time to find a central location to which her clients can come and see her.

Destiny considers what type of space she would need. It would have to be big enough to hold at least three or four tables and a front reception desk. If it has a separate office space for her to have her own office, that would be even better, and it needs to have washrooms for her and her students. She can see it in her mind, filled with plants and a watercooler, with some nice artwork on the walls.

Tomorrow, thinks Destiny. Tomorrow, I will contact a couple of real estate agents and find one who can help me choose some office space in a convenient, central location.

With that decision made, Destiny begins to think about what it would be like to have an actual tutoring center. It's exciting to think of a space dedicated to her passion of helping her students be the best they can be. Excitement runs through her and she can feel butterflies in her stomach.

The phone rings and interrupts Destiny's daydreams. She answers and finds it's Keenan calling.

"Hi, Keenan," she says.

"Hi, Destiny. I was wondering if you would like to get together tomorrow. It's supposed to be a really nice day, pretty warm. I was thinking we could drive around a bit, see some of the area, and then go for a swim. I know a great pool that isn't too far from your place."

Destiny considers. She has a little more free time, now that her Master's degree is done. Maybe it would do her good to get out and socialize.

"Yeah, sure. I'd like that," Destiny replies.

"Awesome!" says Keenan. "Pick you up at noon?"

"Sounds great."

They say their goodbyes and Destiny hangs up. She can leave contacting an agent until Sunday. They aren't going anywhere. Destiny changes into some casual clothes, waters her plants, and then looks for something to watch on TV.

Keenan is prompt on Saturday, showing up right at noon. Destiny is waiting about halfway down the steps of her building when he arrives, and as soon as she sees him, she runs down the remaining steps to greet him. It is nice to see a familiar face from home.

"Hi!" says Keenan and he hugs Destiny.

"Hi," says Destiny.

Keenan opens the car door for her. She gets in and he gets in the driver's side. When he is seated, Keenan says, "I know of a great pool not far from here. We can drive straight over there or drive around the area a bit first."

Destiny opts for a drive first, followed by the pool. She is dressed with her swim suit under her clothes and is traveling light. After seeing some of the sites, they end up at the pool, which is luxuriously warm and not too crowded.

The first thing they do when they get to the pool is to strip down to their suits and take the plunge. It is so refreshing and Destiny just lets herself float as she stares up at the blue sky. There are a few wispy clouds floating across the sky. They look like cotton balls that have been pulled and stretched out of shape. She is enjoying her time relaxing in the water, at least until Keenan decides it would be fun to splash her. Next thing she knows, she and Keenan are having a water fight. Keenan wins.

After they are done swimming, Destiny and Keenan sit in the sun and chat. Destiny brought some snacks and offer Keenan a ham sandwich. Soon, they are both eating. "So, what is happening with you?" asks Keenan between mouthfuls. "You're teaching, right?"

"Yes," replies Destiny, as a small child runs past them, the mother following close behind, calling out to him to walk on the pool deck. "I also have a tutoring business that seems to be growing out of control. I'm actually going to be looking for some office space to open a tutoring center. Then my clients can come to me. I'm getting tired of driving all over the Austin area to work with them."

"That's great, Destiny!" says Keenan. "Dad would be so proud of you, being a business owner and all."

"Well, I learned a lot from him," Destiny says. "I also just got my Master's degree."

"You never cease to amaze," says Keenan. "You must be one of the most educated people from Many, Louisiana."

"Well, I don't know about that. What about you?"

"Well, I graduated from Tullison University. Got a degree in mathematics."

"That's my language," says Destiny.

"Now, I'm looking for work," says Keenan. "Maybe in the financial world or as a statistician. I'm not sure yet, but something that pays well and has the potential for advancement."

"That sounds great," says Destiny. More people have come to the pool and the noise level is rising. Kids are shouting and jumping into the water.

Destiny looks at her cell phone. The time is 2:46. "Oh, my goodness," she says. "I didn't realize it was getting so late. I have a tutoring session at 4:30."

"Well, then we had better get you home," says Keenan, jumping up and extending his hand to Destiny to help her up.

They pack up and head back to Keenan's car. A short while later, they pull into the Destiny's parking lot.

Keenan gets out at the same time as Destiny. "Thanks for today," says Destiny, giving Keenan a hug. "I had fun."

"Glad we could connect," he replies. "Let's do it again soon, except next time, you choose where we go."

"It's a deal."

Destiny walks to her building, while Keenan gets into his car and drives away. Destiny doesn't have much time to change and get going.

As Destiny is unlocking her door, she can hear the phone ringing inside. She hurries and makes it before the phone stops. It's Momma.

"Hi, Momma," says Destiny.

"Hello, sugar. How are ya doin'?"

"I'm fine, Momma. How are y'all?"

"We're fine. You sound out of breath," says Momma.

"I just got in," replies Destiny. "I was just out with Keenan Milestone."

"Is he livin' there?"

"Yes, Momma."

"Now how is he? I just saw his pop the other day."

"He's doing great. But listen, I really have to run because I have a tutoring appointment to get to." The time is 3:37 and Destiny does need to change her clothes and get going. It takes a half an hour to drive across town to get to her client's house.

"Okay, honey," says Momma. "Love you lots."

"I love you, too, Momma. Give Pop a big hug for me."

"You know it," says Momma.

They say their goodbyes and hang up. Destiny has to rush to get changed. She is in such a hurry she almost walks out with her shirt on backwards, but she catches her reflection in the hallway mirror and fixes it.

This is ridiculous, thinks Destiny. She is definitely going to call some agents tomorrow and find one she trusts to help her find a business location. The time to expand Get Your Mind Right Tutoring has come.

Part 3

Chapter 7
Big Truck

D estiny is leaving work one day in early March. She is getting out later than usual and she is tired. All she wants to do is go home, grab a tub of ice cream, and flake out on the sofa to watch Oprah.

Destiny puts her things in the back seat of the car and gets in, but when she tries to start her car, it doesn't work. She tries and tries, but the engine just won't start. Destiny lets her head fall forward until it rests against the steering wheel. This can't be happening.

Destiny gets her phone out and calls a tow truck. At least she is covered for this sort of thing. While she is waiting, Destiny pulls out the math tests she needs to grade and starts working through them.

One hour and 15 math tests later, Destiny can hear the tow truck pull into the school parking lot. She looks at her watch. So much for ice cream and Oprah. Destiny puts away the tests and gets out of the car, taking her things with her.

"Hi," says the driver, getting out of the truck. "What's the problem?"

"It won't start," replies Destiny.

"Okay. My name's Gary, miss. We'll get it to the garage so someone can look at it."

Destiny shakes his hand. "I'm Destiny," she says.

Ten minutes later, Destiny's little green Ford Contour is loaded onto the tow truck and she climbs in beside Gary. They pull out and he asks, "How long have you had your car?"

"A few years," says Destiny. "It's a '97."

"Well, it might not be worth fixin'," he says.

"I suppose. I guess I'll find out soon."

Fifteen minutes later, her car is in a service bay and a mechanic is looking at it. It isn't long before he comes out to speak with Destiny.

"Looks like you need a new engine," he says.

"Really?" asks Destiny.

"Yup. It looks like you've had an oil leak for quite some times and it has damaged the engine. You're looking at close to $3,000. As old as your car is, I don't think it's worth the expense. You'd be better off getting something new."

Destiny bites her lower lip, thinking about what she should do.

"You can leave it here for the night, while you decide," says the mechanic. "That's fine with us."

"I'll do that," says Destiny. "Thanks."

Destiny walks outside and calls Sharia. "Hey, can you come pick me up? My car wouldn't start and I'm at Greg's Supreme Automotive."

"Sure," says Sharia. "I'll be there soon."

It isn't long before Sharia pulls in in her blue Chevy Cavalier. Destiny gets in and they head home.

"Is your car toast?" asks Sharia.

"Yeah, I think so. I'm thinking it's time to get something new."

"I hear that," says Sharia, pulling into their apartment parking lot. "This car is a bucket of junk. Don't know why it hasn't fallen apart yet."

Destiny thanks Sharia and heads up to her apartment. As soon as she gets in, she turns on her computer and finds her local Dodge dealership. She pokes around on their website, looking at all the shiny new cars and trucks. As much as she loves her Ford Contour, those trucks do look fine.

Destiny decides to fill out an online loan application. Within an hour, she is approved and realizes she is going car shopping tomorrow!

Destiny shows up at the dealership as soon as she is off work the next day. She took a taxi there. A sales representative comes out to see Destiny as she is looking at the trucks.

"Hi. I'm Antony. Is there anything I can help you with?"

"Hi, yes. I'm Destiny Sycamores. Last night I went online and was preapproved for a car loan."

"Wonderful! And you're looking at the trucks?"

"I sure am. I grew up with my Pop's truck and I always loved it. This Dodge Ram is really nice."

"Would you like to take it for a test drive?" asks Antony.

"Yes, please!"

Destiny takes the truck out and drives through the neighborhood. She loves the feel of the truck, its power.

When they get back to the dealership, Destiny parks the truck and says, "Sold!"

They go inside and do the paperwork. Destiny has brought everything she needs in terms of proof of income and insurance. She had everything she needs to get her final approval.

Finally, after about 45 minutes of signing papers and waiting, Antony says the truck is hers. They will get it ready for her and she can pick it up on Saturday. That's three agonizing days to wait for her new truck and to get to and from work without a vehicle, but Destiny will manage. She thanks Antony and leaves the dealership feeling great.

Three days later, Destiny is waiting at the dealership doors when it opens. Antony greets her. "You don't mess around, do you?"

Destiny shakes her head and Antony tells her to take a seat while he goes to pull the truck around. Soon, Antony comes in and hands Destiny the keys. "Enjoy your new truck," he says.

Destiny is beyond thrilled. "Thank you so much!"

"It's my pleasure," says Antony, the smile on his face expressing genuine happiness at helping a customer.

She goes outside and gets in her truck. It feels so nice. Granted, she will have to rearrange her budget to accommodate a $400 payment each month, but Destiny knows it is totally worth it.

Now she is going driving! The sun is shining, the day is warm, the breeze is light. The question is where to go. Destiny starts with going through the drive thru and getting coffee and a muffin. She was too excited and in a hurry to eat earlier that morning.

Then she decides she'll go see Katie. Katie lives about 20 miles away and that will give Destiny a chance to really test out her new wheels.

The ride to Katie's house is so smooth and powerful. When Destiny pulls into Katie's driveway, Katie opens her door.

"Oh, Destiny it's you," says Katie. "I saw this truck pull in and didn't know who it was."

"Yup, it's me," says Destiny, smiling broadly as she gets out of her truck.

"Is this yours?" asks Katie.

"It sure is! My car died this week, so I decided it was time to get a new vehicle."

"It's awesome!"

"Wanna go for a ride?" asks Destiny.

"You bet," says Katie. "Just give me a minute."

She runs into the house and is back out quickly, purse in hand.

They pull out and head down the road and onto the highway. With no destination in mind, Destiny opens the sunroof and drives.

Soon, they pull into a roadside diner and go into have some tea and a bite to eat. After they order, Destiny asks, "So, what's up with Julie? I've hardly seen or talked to her lately. I feel like she's been avoiding me."

"Well," says Katie, trying not to look Destiny in the eye.

"Well what?"

"To put it bluntly," says Katie. "Julie is jealous of you."

"Jealous? Of what?"

"Your success with your class, your Master's degree, the conference you're going to. Everything!"

"But why? She could do all those things, too."

Katie looks at Destiny, her expression serious. "Listen, Destiny. You're successful and brilliant and you seriously don't rub it in, but you are a dynamo and hard to keep up with, sometimes."

"I just work hard, that's all."

"I know you do," says Katie. "You deserve everything you have, but Julie struggles with organization and time and right now it's not feasible for her to go to school and do all these extra things."

Destiny is silent as their food and drinks are delivered. Then Katie says, "Don't worry about it. Julie will come around. She just needs to think things through and she'll be happy for you. You'll see. She might be the jealous type, but she is also loyal to a fault."

"I hope so," says Destiny. "I miss her."

"I know. And I miss the three of us getting together for karaoke."

Destiny giggles at that. When they are done, Destiny realizes she needs to get going. She drives Katie home and drops her off. Destiny gives Katie a big hug. "Thanks for the talk."

"Anytime!"

Then Destiny pulls out and boss-hogs the highway the whole way home.

Chapter 8

Conference

Late March has arrived and Destiny is putting her suitcase and briefcase in her truck. She has packed everything she will need while she is away at the conference. She has done her best to keep herself busy over the past few weeks so she hasn't been constantly thinking about the conference, but it has been difficult because she is so excited. She feels like a little kid on Christmas morning!

Destiny has a substitute teacher taking her class for the rest of the week and early next week and she has arranged for her tutoring students to work without her for the few days she is gone. For the first time in a long time, Destiny is free of obligation for a few days and can relax and enjoy herself.

Destiny was given the option to fly to Arizona, but she wanted to drive. She is still enjoying her new truck and wants to chew up some highway with it. Besides, driving is a great way to see the country. You can't see nearly as much from the air.

Destiny gets on the road by 8:00 am and drives through Texas that day, finding a nice motel in the outskirts of El Paso to spend the night. The scenery along the way has been stunning. She has never been this far west before and the desert is such a sight to see. It's like there is nothing and everything all at once. The desert is such a huge space that is loud in its silence and isolation.

By the time she arrives in Phoenix the next day, it is just early afternoon. Destiny finds her hotel, which is where the conference is being held, and checks in. Her room is gorgeous! Destiny has not stayed in a hotel very many times in her life and this is a particularly nice hotel.

The queen-size bed has a brightly colored flowered quilt on it and there is a huge TV and a desk. The bathroom is clean and bright with a great big bathtub. But it's the view Destiny loves most of all. She is on the sixth floor of the hotel, which is high enough to give her a spectacular view of the city. It is truly breathtaking.

With time to kill before registration and the opening dinner reception, Destiny decides to spend some time by the pool. She unpacks her suitcase and changes into her bathing suit. Then she grabs a towel and heads down. She finds a lounge chair in the sun and orders an ice tea. The hot sun and cool drink are such a great combination that Destiny finds her mind drifting away until she almost falls asleep. Then a child jumps into the pool and splashes Destiny, which wakes her right up.

"So sorry!" says the child's mother.

"It's no problem," says Destiny, feeling very refreshed. Maybe it's time for a swim, she thinks.

After a dip in the pool and some more time laying in the sun, Destiny decides she should go up and shower so she can get ready for her evening. When she gets to her floor, she gets off the elevator and turns down the hallway to walk to her room. She is just about to open her door when the door across the hall opens and out walks Principal Easton.

"Hello, Principal Easton," says Destiny.

"Please, call me Tejay," he replies. "We aren't at school right now."

"Sounds fine, Tejay. How was your trip here?"

"It was fine, fine. Nice flight. Looks like we're neighbors."

"Looks like," says Destiny.

They stand there for a moment in silence and Destiny finally says, "Well, I had better get cleaned up and changed for tonight."

"Yes, you do that. I'll see you down stairs in a while."

A half an hour later, with a fabulous red dress on, Destiny goes down to register for the conference.

Then she finds her colleagues. Tejay welcomes her to the table and tells Destiny she looks very nice. He has saved a seat for her right next to his. Destiny takes her seat and has a lovely dinner with her colleagues. Then she decides to hit the casino and Tejay joins her. He has never been to a casino before and he is excited to see what it's like.

By the end of the evening, Destiny has won $300. What a great start to the conference weekend!

The next day, Destiny walks out of the last session for the day, a stimulating discussion on professional learning communities. She is famished. One of the teachers she has gotten to know during the day, Debbie Axton, comes up to her.

"Hey, Destiny. A bunch of us are heading out for dinner at the Authentic Mexican Restaurant. Wanna join us?"

"Sounds great," says Destiny. "Just give me a minute to run up to my room and grab my purse."

"Okay, we'll wait in the lobby."

Destiny gets upstairs, grabs her purse, and is closing the door to her room when Tejay comes down the hallway.

"Destiny, there you are," he says. "I was looking for you."

"Really?"

"Yes, I wanted to ask you to dinner. I know of a nice Chinese restaurant we can go to."

Destiny is stunned. "Oh, well thank you, Tejay, but I've already made plans."

"Ah, I see," he says, his face turning scarlet. "Of course, that's fine. You go and enjoy yourself. I should probably get some work done, anyway."

"Okay," says Destiny. "Enjoy your evening."

"You, too," he replies and then he shoots into his room.

When Destiny gets back down to the lobby, she meets up with the group and they head out. They get two taxis between them and Destiny sits in the back of one with Debbie.

"You know," says Destiny, "I think my principal has a crush on me."

"Really?" asks Debbie.

"Yeah. He just asked me out to dinner."

"You sure it wasn't a professional invitation?"

"No," says Destiny. "It didn't seem that way. He was pretty flustered when I said I had other plans."

"Well, that's awkward," says Debbie.

"No kidding!" says Destiny, but as they drive she sees herself in the future, in much the same role as Tejay. She knows he is dedicated to helping teachers the same way she will be and she knows his feelings for her won't be a problem.

When Destiny gets back to the hotel that night, she is stuffed full of amazing food and very happy. She had this wonderful Mexican soup called Pozole and then she had chicken enchiladas. By the time she was done she had no room left for dessert.

When they arrive back at the hotel, everyone heads inside, except Destiny.

"You coming in?" asks Debbie.

"Not quite yet," answers Destiny. "It's just so nice out. I think I want to enjoy the evening air for a while."

"Mind if I join you?"

"Not at all."

Destiny and Debbie stand near the fountain in front of the hotel. The air is a little cooler and quite pleasant now that it's evening and the sun is beginning to set. Even though the buildings of downtown Phoenix are blocking some of the skyline, Destiny is able to see the sky turning a brilliant red.

"It's stunning, isn't it?" says Debbie.

"It sure is."

Then they just watch in silence because there is simply no need to say anything when such beauty is present.

Once the sun has set, Destiny and Debbie go inside and get in the elevator. They say goodbye when Debbie gets off on the fifth floor. Destiny continues up to her floor and heads to her room. She is tired and needs to pack up and get ready to check out tomorrow. The conference goes until mid-afternoon, but Destiny has to check out by 11:00 am.

Once in her room, Destiny packs up what she can and gets ready for bed. Then she decides to look for something to watch on TV. *Grey's Anatomy* and *24* are on, so she chooses *Grey's Anatomy* and watches it.

After she turns the TV off, Destiny settles down to go to sleep, but sleep doesn't come easily. She is still thinking about Tejay. She knows she needs to keep her end professional and she is sure he will do the same.

Destiny is also thinking about the beauty of Arizona. It's most certainly hot for March, but it is the desert, after all. As Destiny snuggles into her bed, she realizes she wishes that it was her own bed, but here in Arizona. Wouldn't that be something?

Then a vision comes to Destiny. She is in Arizona, but it's in the future. She is older. She has moved to Arizona to open a healing center. She doesn't get a clear glimpse of the center, so she really doesn't know what it will look like, but she knows it is going to happen. She also knows that she will be able to enjoy all the desert sunsets and sunrises she wants one day, something she will always cherish.

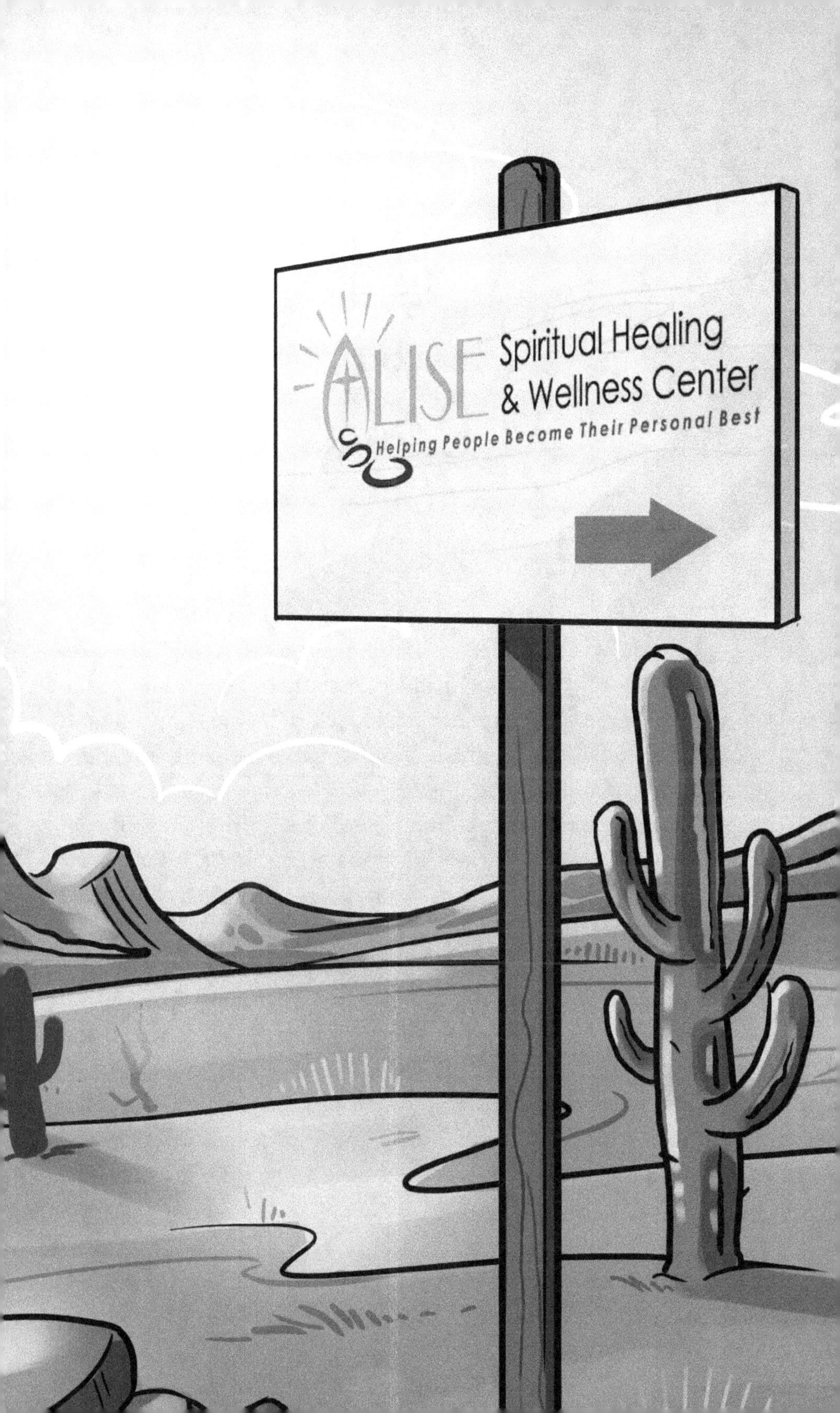
ALISE
Spiritual Healing
& Wellness Center
Helping People Become Their Personal Best

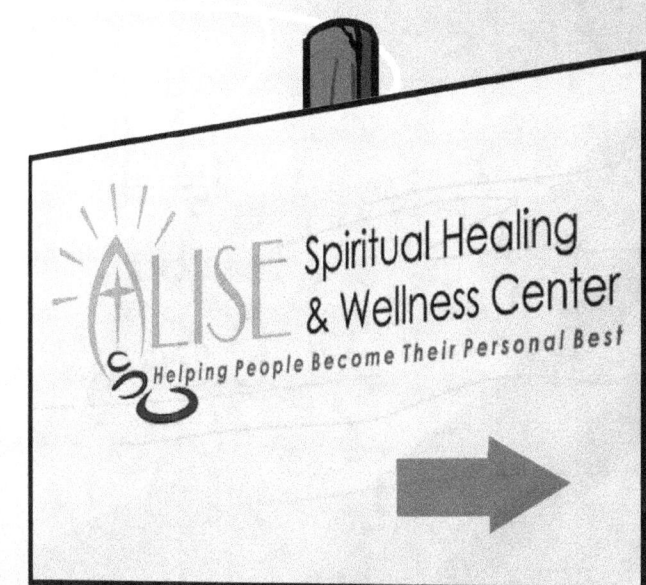

Chapter 9

Book

The sun is out and it's a fine Saturday morning. It's been two weeks since the conference and Destiny has been thinking about what she learned there. As she sits on the steps of her apartment building, enjoying the morning sun and a cup of coffee, she begins to write down her experiences, both as a teacher and as a tutor.

Suddenly, someone shouts up, "Hey, Destiny!" It's Sharia. She comes up the stairs and stops a couple of steps below where Destiny is sitting. "What are you up to today?" Sharia asks.

"Hi, Sharia," says Destiny. "Relaxing this morning, then I have some tutoring appointments this afternoon. You?"

"I'm outta here. A day at the pool with Q. What's with the notebook?"

"Oh, that. Just been thinking about my experience as a teacher, writing some stuff down. You know, I really don't think teachers have the resources they need to do their job properly. What do you think?"

"First, I think you have a funny way of relaxing," says Sharia. "But I think you're right. We are stretched too thin and it can be hard to find the time to get students the extra help they need."

"I agree. I think I might write a book about it."

"That's a great idea!" says Sharia. "I'd buy that book. And I'd recommend it to all my teaching friends."

"Thanks," says Destiny.

"So, I take it your tutoring business is going well," says Sharia.

"Very. I'm actually looking for some office space to have a centralized location. Then my students can come to me and I will be able to serve more people who need the help."

"Wow! That's amazing. I know who to send my students to if they need extra help that we can't give them."

"Thanks," says Destiny. "I'd appreciate referrals."

"Okay, well I have to get out of here. Enjoy relaxing," Sharia says with a wink.

"Bye," says Destiny.

Destiny finishes her coffee and is about to get up and go inside when her cell phone rings. It's Keenan so she answers it. "Hi, Keenan."

"Hi," he says. His voice sounds a little off, different than usual. He almost sounds guilty, like he's done something wrong.

Destiny ignores the sinking feeling in her stomach. "What's up?" she asks, sounding cheerful.

"I was calling to tell you that I'm moving to Dallas."

Destiny is stunned. She knew Keenan was looking for work, but she thought he was staying in the Austin area. That's what he had said he was going to do.

"Oh," she says. "Did you get a job there?"

"Yeah, I got an accounting job with a great company. I'm sorry, but I got the offer and couldn't pass it up. You know? Gotta go where the work is."

"Of course," says Destiny. "No, I understand. Thanks for letting me know. When do you leave?"

"I'm moving down next week. I have a friend I can stay with until I get my own place."

"That's great, Keenan. I'm happy for you. I bet your dad is, too."

"Yeah," Keenan hesitates. "He sure is. Well, I have to go. I have a lot to do."

"Yeah, me, too," says Destiny. "Bye."

"See ya," says Keenan. Then he hangs up.

Destiny still doesn't feel right about that conversation, but there isn't much she can do. Besides, she needs to get ready for her tutoring appointments. She collects her things and goes inside to get ready to go.

Later that afternoon, with her tutoring sessions done for the day, Destiny is feeling depressed. Keenan is a connection from home that she relied on. Of course, she is much more adjusted to living in Austin than she was when she moved here, but she still has her moments when she misses home desperately. With the news of Keenan leaving, one of those moods has settled over Destiny.

As she is driving home, Destiny decides to change direction at the last minute. She heads to the mall. She needs a break and the mall is a place she likes to go sometimes when she is missing home. It reminds her of home because of her years working at the jewelry store.

When she gets to the mall and parks, she makes her way to the food court. There is just something universal about a food court in a mall. There are always the same restaurants and it always has the same feel, no matter what city you're in.

Destiny goes from some Japanese food. She finds a seat and watches the people go by as she eats. She feels it's nice to get out sometimes and go somewhere where she isn't alone, yet she can be by herself.

Destiny takes her time eating and then she cleans up her table. She sees some tables with trays and food wrappers still on them. She has never understood why some people don't clean up after themselves. Momma would never let her leave her garbage behind for the custodians to clean up. "Those folks got enough to do cleaning up after people," she would say. "They don't need to pick up your trash, too."

Destiny has been planning on going rug shopping for a while now. She needs something nice for her living room floor. So, she heads to the department store and goes to the appropriate section. There is a salesperson there and he welcomes her. "Hi there. Is there anything I can help you with?"

"I'm looking for a rug for my living room," says Destiny.

"Well, you're in the right place. These rugs are brand new. Just came in today."

Destiny looks at them. They are really nice, very colorful. She has worked hard to make her apartment look nice. She feels that how her home looks is a reflection of her level of success. She wants to be successful, so she makes her apartment look like she is successful.

"These are really nice," says Destiny, looking through the different colors and patterns.

"Are you looking for something more subdued?"

"No," Destiny replies, "I definitely want some color."

"How about this one?"

The one he shows her has brightly colored flowers on it. It would really liven up her apartment.

"Yes," says Destiny. "I really this this one. I'll take it."

"Wonderful," says the salesperson. "If you want, I'll take it up to the cash register. Feel free to keep shopping if you like. It will be waiting for you when you're ready."

"That's great. Thanks."

Destiny takes some time to wander around the store. There really isn't anything else she needs, but she doesn't feel like going home just yet.

Her home does look nice, but all of a sudden it hits Destiny. She doesn't need to make her home look like she is successful. She *is* successful! Destiny realizes how much of a success she has made of her life. She is in a place she loves, she is well-educated, and she is working with children and helping them to be better people, to be everything they can be, so they have the same opportunities she has had.

Nothing could be more rewarding. Destiny has created the life that she wants. And now she is going to expand her tutoring business and write a book that will allow her to help other teachers and educators help children create the lives they want.

With this realization, Destiny feels better. She goes and pays for her rug and takes it to her truck. Then she drives home and when she gets the rug up to her apartment, moves the furniture, lays the rug, and puts everything back into place, she is amazed. The look of her home is just how she feels inside. Successful, full of color and potential, and ready to do more with her life.

Chapter 10

Epilogue

With the arrival of summer just around the corner, Destiny has grabbed hold of the opportunity to write her book. Plus, she will get to go home and visit her family this summer, something she desperately wants to do.

Even though her tutoring business is thriving, with her Master's degree done, Destiny has the time to write. She also wants to work on the Secret Sisters Club. She has some big plans for that and she is hoping that she will have the opportunity to start the club up in the fall, when the students come back to school. Maybe she could hold a fall dinner event or something like that.

At the end of the school day one day, three weeks before school is out for the summer, Katie stops by Destiny's classroom.

"Hey there," says Katie.

"Hi," says Destiny.

"Listen, I was thinking that once school is out, we could go on a little weekend getaway. I really want to go to Houston and see what it's like. You in?"

"Yeah, that sounds like fun!" says Destiny.

"Awesome. How about we plan it for two weeks after school is done for the year? It will give us time to wrap things up here before we go."

"Sounds like a great plan," says Destiny. "What about Julie? Do you think she'll go?"

"I don't know," replies Katie. "I can ask her."

"I really hope she comes. I'd like to mend fences with her, although I really don't know how. I don't feel like I did anything wrong. How can I apologize when I haven't done anything?"

Destiny still hasn't been able to get through to Julie. Julie speaks to Destiny when she starts a conversation, but she doesn't make any real effort to carry on their friendship.

"I know," says Katie. "Listen, I'll talk to her, ask her to come. Maybe she'll come around."

"Okay, thanks," says Destiny.

"See, ya," says Katie.

Destiny sits there thinking about Julie and their relationship. Then she realizes it's not just Julie. No one has treated her the same way since she was given her own classroom and gone to the conference. Destiny doesn't understand. She certainly didn't do anything wrong, but for some reason other people seem to feel threatened by her success.

It's a difficult thing to comprehend, but Destiny has no intention of slowing down and giving in to the unjustified feelings of others. Destiny feels that every person is capable of making their life better in some way. She has worked hard to be where she is and she doesn't have to apologize for that.

Still, she does miss her friendship with Julie. Maybe Katie can convince her to go on the trip and help turn things around. Destiny packs up to head home for the day. She has some writing to do!

About the Author

Alicia Linelle Holland was born and raised in Many, Louisiana and got her middle name after her mother, Vera Linelle. When Alicia was in middle school, she started the Secret Sister Club that you read about in the Linelle Destiny Book Series. Alicia Holland has been working towards bringing back the Secret Sister Club as she embarks upon quite an interesting life and spiritual journey. At age 26, she earned her Doctorate in Education so that she can be in a position to help others believe in themselves and go far. At age 31, Dr. Alicia Holland opened a Not for Profit, Alise Spiritual Healing & Wellness Center and was officially ordained as a Minister. As a Transformational Life Coach, Professor, Author, Speaker, and Minister, Dr. Holland travels the World sharing her message: "You are Loved, You are Valued, and You are Competent.

Dr. Alicia Holland has two beautiful daughters, ages 7 and 9, who travels the World with her and are active participants in the Secret Sister Club Mentoring Program. She and her family resides in Austin, Texas and are currently looking for a new puppy.

Dr. Holland is available for speaking engagements and can be reached at support@thesecretsistersclub.com or support@iglobaleducation.com.